D0519564

# Hot Flush

### by

## Helen FitzGerald

WITHDRAWN

993397519 6

| GLOUCESTERSHIRE COUNTY COUNCIL | |
|---|---|
| 9933975196 | |
| Bertrams | 11/02/2012 |
| AF | £5.99 |
| CR | |

First published in 2011 in Great Britain by
Barrington Stoke Ltd
18 Walker Street, Edinburgh, EH3 7LP

www.barringtonstoke.co.uk

Copyright © 2011 Helen FitzGerald

The moral right of the author has been asserted in
accordance with the Copyright, Designs and
Patents Act 1988

ISBN: 978-1-84299-866-3

Printed in Great Britain by Bell and Bain

For Joe Cesci

With special thanks to our readers:

Catherine Graham
Seán P. Hurl
Janice McAvoy
Theresa McClung
Donald McKay
Derek Sinclair

# Chapter 1

Jim Bain was in love. Head over heels in love. It wasn't a woman he loved. He wasn't the kind of wimp who went all soft over a girl. And anyway, no woman could whisper into his brain from over a hundred yards, "Come to me, touch me, stroke me, get inside me." No woman had the sleek black charm of that Alfa Romeo for example, the one that some knob had parked in front of the newsagents last Sunday, the one that told him he had to *Come, come, come here and be one with me. Now!*

Like sex or eating, it was hard to recall the best part after he'd done it. Was it sizing up the job, knowing he was about to be satisfied as he walked across the street? Was it breaking into the car, the method of attack? Or the ride itself, spinning and thrusting along the streets? Perhaps the happy sigh at the end, as he parked the Alfa near a deserted factory on the Clyde, handed it over to his buyer, patted the bonnet goodbye, and then left to go home.

Ah, it was *all* good. No part better than another. Each added to the buzz that made him feel alive, made his cheeks rosy, made him run with joy along the riverside yelling *Ha!* He'd done it. Screw the rich bastard who owned it, who'd no doubt come out of the shop with *The Times* under his arm to find his car gone and yelled into his latest iPhone, "Come now, I say! Some Ned's stolen my Alfa!" Screw the polis who'd no doubt return the car to its owner in his suburban semi within the week. Then they would add the theft to some poor guy's charge sheet to make things nice and neat. Screw them all. Life was great. The only thing that'd make it better was chips with cheese. Oh, and to not have that bloody group to go to tomorrow.

He'd been on probation for nine months

now, and going to the group for three months. Once a week for two whole hours he'd sit in a semi-circle in front of some flabby old cow who knew nothing about him. Some posh English bitch who believed she'd been called by God to save him and the others just like him – poor and disenfranchised and aching for a helping hand. To save him, she had to dig into his past, two hours each time, dig, dig, dig. Into the death of his grandfather – the only person who'd ever loved him. Into his parents who'd never worked and who'd drunk and smoked themselves to death, leaving him an orphan. Into the under-resourced school he'd hardly gone to. Into the children's homes he'd run away from. Into the self-esteem he probably lacked. Into the conscience he *obviously* lacked. Blah, blah, blah.

The chips were good. The cheese was good. He'd sleep well that night, he thought, as he walked towards his block. He'd take the lift to the 14th floor, lock the door of his furnished flat for the homeless – one of the perks of having a do-gooding probation officer – and dream about his past love, and of his next. A

Mini perhaps? Or a gleaming yellow Bugatti motor bike? But then he never knew what might appear as if by magic and beckon him.

Jim woke at 4am. The grass always got him to sleep, but never for long. It was mid summer and the sun was already making it impossible to get back to sleep. He should ask the old bird about black-out blinds at the group. Surely lack of sleep was one of the "reasons for his criminal acts".

He watched TV for four hours, then remembered his homework. He had to fill in a sheet for the group. He dug it out of his jeans pocket, flattened the folds with his hand, and filled in the form as fast as he could.

**Factors Leading Up To The Crime** – *What happened before the offence for which you were later placed on Probation? Take yourself back to the moment just before you committed the crime.*
*Where are you?*

Old Rutherford Road.

*Who are you with?*

No one. I don't need no one.

*What time is it?*

8.

*Have you eaten?*

No.

*Have you had anything to drink?*

Aye.

*Have you taken any drugs?*

Just dope is all.

*What were you doing an hour ago?*

Watching the TV.

*What are you doing now?*

Just going for a walk. Nothing wrong with that.

*And how are you feeling?*


What a load of shite. He hadn't even committed the crime they were asking him about. His charge sheet was filled with other people's crimes, as other people's were filled with his. The polis didn't seem to bother much about getting it right. He didn't answer the last question, folded the page and shoved it back in his jeans pocket.

The group met in the social work block at the end of the road. He strolled past a mountain of rubble, twenty metres high, the remains of the 60's high rise block he grew up in. The one his father drank in till he turned yellow and dropped dead, the one his mother collapsed in one night when the fags finally got the last of her lungs, the one they blasted with dynamite a month ago as the city watched, popcorn in hand.

"No smoking here," said the security guard as Jim entered the ground floor reception area.

"Aye, I know," Jim said, hurling his still-lit roll-up out of the window and walking into the tiny lift.

"Oy! In the bin, you ..." The lift doors had shut before the security guard could finish.

When Jim got to the third floor, the place was heaving. Six of his fellow probationers were already waiting on seats in reception. Two toddlers were yelling around the sad excuse for a play area – a gym mat and two big rubber squares oozing foam – while their mothers complained to each other about them. Two meth' users sweated as they waited for the clinic, and a blind guy stood at the large reception desk asking the grumpy receptionist for a form to get a bus pass.

"Hey, Jim," one of the probationers said.

"Hey." Jim did not make eye contact. These guys were not his mates.

"Hi, guys!" The seven young offenders all turned round and rolled their eyes. It was Eileen. 45 years old. Light denim Marks and Spencer's jeans, pink blouse that was too small for her enormous (but not in a good way) tits, and a black cardigan covered in some kind of white mank. She had greasy thin hair that stuck out stiffly at the back, and ballet-style shoes that you could tell stank of sweat just by looking at them. If this woman had ever been good looking, it must have been a long time ago. She was one of the least attractive women Jim had ever seen in his life.

# Chapter 2

Eileen's hair was a mess. She knew it was a mess. She wished it wasn't. She wished her hair was thick and brown and shiny like it had been ten years earlier. Why had her hair let her down like this? Why had it given her the Vicky like everything else gave her two fingers nowadays? Her hair seemed to be saying, *Bugger off, Eileen. I'm not going to make things nicer for you. You fat old bag.*

But today her hair was really bad. It was the wind that did it. Glasgow is not very windy – but when you are rocking back and forth in the side car of your husband's new Harley

Davidson, it's a different matter. When the new oversized helmet has fallen to the back of your neck and the strap is strangling you as your husband takes the slip road off the Kingston Bridge with a terrifying tilt – then, Glasgow is very windy. As a result, Eileen's hair travelled behind her all the way from Jordanhill to the Gorbals and remained behind her all day.

Stupid bike. What was wrong with the huge 25-year-old Volvo she'd bought after college and loved? What was wrong with Richard's near-new Golf GT? What made him think it was OK to trade them both in like that without asking her?

"Darling, come and look," he'd said a few nights before, and Eileen had closed the roast chicken-filled oven (Fridays were roast chicken) and followed him through the connecting door into the double garage.

"Isn't it gorgeous!" he'd said, not needing a reply. "I waited months for the sidecar to arrive. I'm thinking of naming it Eileen, or perhaps Moppet. What do you think?"

She wasn't the kind of person to get cross. She didn't get cross when her father berated her for doing social work. ("For God's sake, woman, you could do Law with those marks. You'll earn next to nothing. What are you, a socialist or something?") She didn't get cross when her parents sold their house and moved to Provence and never invited her to stay, or visited her in Glasgow. ("Why are you living there? In the rain? With all those miserable Scots?") She didn't even get cross when she realised she had married a man exactly like her father – different name, different accent, but otherwise exactly the same.

So Eileen didn't get cross about the bike. She ate the roast chicken slowly and breathed carefully. She spent the weekend cutting the hedge. She looked on the bright side. Perhaps she would enjoy taking it for a ride. She suggested this on Sunday night as they finished their sausages and mash (Sundays: sausages and mash).

"You mean you ride it? It's very large, you know. Why do you think I paid £8,000 for the side car?" Richard said.

Perhaps they would enjoy going into the country next weekend, she suggested, as images of what she might have spent the £8,000 on whirled angrily before her (a trip to Ethiopia to visit an orphanage for example). They still had babies for adoption there.

"The country! Whatever's in the country? Why don't we stop talking about the bike for a moment? Why don't you clear up here and we can have some hanky panky?"

"The doctor says I shouldn't have sex," Eileen said, piling up the dishes.

The doctor had said nothing of the sort. In fact, the doctor had said, "You should enjoy sex now that you know you can't get pregnant any more ... Now that you're changing"

*Changing*, it sounded a nice, cosy word, but really meant your insides *shrivelling up as you neared the end of your pointless life.*

"The doctor says it's dangerous," she said again as Richard undid his trousers and got ready anyway.

"What about a curry tomorrow?" Eileen asked. She would have been wise to have waited for a better moment before making such a daring suggestion, but she thought Richard might give in as she splayed to let him in. She thought he might lose himself in the moment and agree to ordering a carry-out.

"What?" he huffed from his doggy position, the one he liked best as he could imagine her different from behind. He could close his eyes and pump her as if she was the 23-year-old girl she used to be – the one he fell in love with at the tennis club. Slim, with pretty blue eyes, a sweet looking face, and a short white skirt that bounced off her lean smooth legs. Or better still, he could imagine she was Jane, his new secretary, who'd thrust her bosom at him as she leaned down to present him the 2008-2009 tax return documents for A.C. Plumbing.

"There's a new Indian in Great Western Road," Eileen told him.

"But," he said, "mince ... Ah ... Mince ... hold on ..."

The dog had jumped on the bed and was licking Eileen's face. She hated the cutesy white

Scottish terrier. Richard had presented it to her in the same way he'd presented the Harley. "Come look," he'd said one Friday a few months prior. "Her name's Moppet."

Eileen looked on the bright side. She had no proper friends, and she wondered if the dog might become one. Everyone at college and at work seemed to hate her because of her background, her accent and her large house in the leafy green suburbs, complete with right wing husband. She hadn't managed to make a single friend on the Beginner's Italian or Cake Making classes she'd taken up since it had become clear that she would never be a mother. She and had lost touch with the girls she knew at boarding school (Lucy, Amy and Fifi, who all had at least two surnames each and most likely now had sons with three or four surnames, and first names like Harry, Rupert and Christian). Perhaps, Eileen thought hopefully, Moppet would become her best friend, removing the desperate need she sometimes felt to have the kind of female friend that women have on TV. One who could share regular cappuccinos in trendy city cafes,

13

who would phone to arrange weekly outings to the cinema/theatre/restaurant, or – best of all – would just phone for no reason ("I just needed to hear your voice," they might say) very late at night. Of course the dog wouldn't phone her, but Moppet might long for Eileen's company. She might snuggle into her lap on the sofa at night. She might love her for herself.

When Moppet first arrived, Eileen decided to take her new Best Friend Forever for a walk. But Moppet had no interest in this new friendship. Despite being meek and loving and lovable and cute as a button when she was with Richard, Moppet had the unlikely doggy skill of transforming herself into a monster when her master wasn't looking. As such, Moppet would narrow her eyes and snarl, showing sharp jagged teeth that snapped hungrily at chunks of Eileen's body. She foamed at the mouth and resisted the gentle coaxing of the lead. She peed on Eileen's left leg, then on her right. She did a long slithery poo on the doorstep of the newsagents, just as Eileen's handsome neighbour, Matt, walked out with his milk. Matt had flirted with her in the early years but now saved his flirting for the yummy mummies who'd recently arrived in the area to take advantage of the excellent schools. By the end of that first fateful walk, Moppet had made it clear that she would never, ever, be Eileen's friend.

Right now, the dog was licking Eileen's face in time with Richard's thrusts. Eileen could taste thick slimy organic dog-biscuit saliva as Richard grabbed her hair for the grand final which went like this:

"Hold on, hold on … yes … yes … Oh, Jane …"

"Eileen!" she corrected her husband mid doggy lick.

"Don't ruin it!" Richard wheezed.

He finished with her in the same way that he finished with his morning *Daily Mail* – that's that done, put it down, fold it, pat it – then he sat up, grabbed Moppet and kissed her nose. "You are gorgeous so you are! Yes you are!"

Still on all fours, head in the pillow, Eileen rubbed the dog ooze from her face and let out a muffled sigh.

Pulling on his not-so-white, not-so-brief briefs, Richard turned to Eileen and added, "You know Mondays are mince."

Richard had never been very good at changing plans.


Richard hadn't dog-proofed the garden yet. There was no front fence and Moppet could easily escape. So when he went to work Richard left the back door to the garage open and tied Moppet to a workbench at the back of the garage with a bright green stretchy lead. The lead was so long that Moppet could reach all parts of the garage and the back garden. Richard had converted the garage into a doggy playroom. Inside, the dog enjoyed a mass of pillows, balls and squeaky, squealy plastic toys. As Eileen and Richard entered this doggy-hotel on Monday morning, they noticed that Moppet had already taken to sleeping in the side car.

"Oh, look at you! Look at you!" Richard said, picking up and cuddling his fluffy love. "Are you hungry? Do you want some of this?"

Before Eileen could protest, Richard had taken the brown paper bag from her hand, unwrapped her ham sandwich, and given it to the dog. As Moppet ate Eileen's lunch, Richard closed the inner door to the house and locked it, opened the back door of the garage and put a brick in front of it, and tied one end of Moppet's lead to the collar and the other to the legs of the work bench.

"Bye, honey, bye bye!" he said, putting on his helmet and handing Eileen her huge head-piece and her set of keys. "I've put a spare key to the bike on there," he told her. "I'm trusting you with it. Guard it with your life," he said.

"But the seat's covered in dog hair!" Eileen said, trying without success to brush the seat of the side car with her hand. Richard didn't care. Richard didn't care about anything to do with Eileen. He revved his manly engine and they screeched out of the garage.

Pressing the button on her key, Eileen watched as the automatic front doors of the garage closed, leaving Moppet alone for the day.

"Tea and train money," Richard said as he dropped her at her office. Eileen took the five pound note, undid her helmet, placed it back in the side car, and got out. As Richard roared off, she tried to clean the hair from her black cardigan, but it refused to move. She gave up, entered the office block, and gave the security guard a cheerful greeting which she did not feel. She only had twenty minutes before her boys arrived. Enough time to check her dookit for messages and any new tasks, grab a cup of coffee, and get the room ready for the group.

Each week the same feeling of dread took over. Her workmates not only looked down on her but were not shy about letting her know this. Her boss, Jennifer, barely noticed her presence as she walked past her office – "There are three new court reports coming your way," was all she said this particular morning. As Eileen entered her own office, shared with three others, her team members were chatting about the newest TV reality show. They made no attempt to bring her into the conversation (mind you, Eileen never watched reality television. Real life reality was enough to cope with). The office staff gave one word responses to her chirpy "Good mornings". As for the young offenders, they detested her accent and the power she had over them. One wrong move, and she could send them back to jail.

"Hi, guys," she said, gathering her strength, trying not to show her fear. "Did you all have a good weekend?"

# Chapter 3

*Did we all have a good weekend? What would she know about a good weekend?* Jim wondered as he followed her up the stairs and into the group work room.

As always, Jim took the end seat in the semi-circle. The six other boys fidgeted as Eileen closed the door, turned to a fresh sheet of paper on the flip chart and wrote at the top "Events leading up to the crime." The mass fidgeting was partly due to utter boredom, partly due to the thought of two more hours of utter boredom, and party due to a frantic need for a fix. Three of the seven were using heroin, the other three had converted to the legal drug, methadone. Jim was the only one who hadn't given in to the hard stuff – but this wasn't the only thing that made him different from the others. Jim believed he offended for good reasons. He offended because he loved cars. He offended because it made his pulse race. It wasn't about getting money for drugs. He wasn't some desperate junkie no-hoper. He had a plan. And he was so, so, close to getting there.

There was always some daft warm-up exercise. This time, the boys had to take it in turns to say how they were feeling.

*I'm Martin and I'm feeling um … worried.*

*I'm Rab and I'm feeling worried as well.*

*I'm Jonesey* (Jonesey clawed his crotch) *and I'm feeling … myself …* Everyone but Eileen laughed.

*Yeah, I'm worried,* said Chris.

*I'm Ray and I'm feeling worried.*

*I'm Chas and I'm worried.*

*I'm Jim and I'm feeling bored.*

"Thanks for your honesty, boys. Now …

21

today we're going to focus on ..."

Seven boys stopped fidgeting, stopped breathing. *Please not me, please not me ...*

"Jim ..."

*Fuck* said Jim out loud.

"Excuse me? What did you say?" Eileen asked.

"I said 'fuck', but it was by mistake," Jim said.

"What did you mean to say?" Eileen asked.

"I meant to say 'fuck'."

"So it wasn't a mistake?"

"I meant to say it to myself."

"Oh, dear, Jim. Remember last week I gave you a second written warning for being late again? You got that letter, yes?"

"Aye." He was using the envelope to keep his hash stash in. He was running out of it anyway.

"Now I'm afraid I'm going to have to remind you of our rules, Jim. No swearing, no fights, no racist remarks ... We are all here under the orders of the court. As such, we must act with respect towards each other. Respect is the key. Respect the law. Respect the court. Respect each other. If you continue to break the rules you will find you have run out of warnings."

"Oh, dear," Jim said, getting her tone of voice spot on.

"Could you take out your homework sheet, please, Jim? Today we are going to take a look at what happened just before your offence was committed."

"Next week we will look at the *offence* itself. The week after that will be all about the *consequences*. But today we are looking at what happened before the index offence, in other words the offence for which you were put on probation. What led to the crime? Jim, I want you to take yourself back ... Am I right in thinking, you stole the vehicle at 8.30pm on a Saturday? Imagine it's 8pm on the night it happened. Give us some words ... brainstorm ... free your mind ... What are you feeling?"

"Fucked if I know," Jim said. "Cannae think of the words."

"OK, now, I'm sorry, but you are not co-operating and I'm on the brink of having to consider giving you a final, final warning, Jim." Eileen flipped the huge papers on her chart till she found the sheet titled "Contract – Ground Rules". She pointed at the words "No Swearing" with her red felt tip pen and prodded it. *That was the way she'd prod the chest of her husband if he failed to take out the rubbish in time,* Jim thought.

"This is bullshit."

Jim was up for a fight.

Eileen had no choice. The Scottish Office made it clear that she had no choice. Three warnings and you're done. Eileen felt unhappy about the power she held over Jim. She hadn't done social work to have power. She'd done it to try and make things more even. But here it was, and it was making her face hot and damp with sweat. It was causing her hands to shake.

All of the boys, except Jim, did indeed seem worried now.

"I'm afraid I'm left with no choice but to send you back to court, Jim Bain. I shall tell them you have broken your contract, that you have not co-operated with the instructions of your supervising officer. You have behaved in a rude and anti-social manner in group work. I shall say that I believe that to keep you in custody is the only choice left to the court. I am going to send the report today. Soon, Jim, you will be locked up in Polmont Young Offender's Institution. For now, though, I would like you to leave so I can work with these other young men, young men who do want to lead law abiding lives."

Jim didn't move.

"Is there some reason you are not leaving the room, Mr Bain?"

He didn't answer her.

"Is there some reason why you are not interested in changing your ways?"

A pause, then, "Well yes, there is."

"Then make the most of the free time you have left and tell us what that reason is."

"OK," Jim began, "brainstorm, imagine, free your mind ... It's 8pm. You're looking for a car. You can feel your heart beat. You feel alive.

It feels better than sex. Can you imagine that? Have you ever felt like that?"

Silence. A large drop of sweat had fallen into Eileen's left eye. She tried not to blink, but couldn't, and the drop fell to her cheek like a tear.

"Thought not."

"You should think about the consequences of your actions," Eileen said, wiping her face.

Sweat had taken over her entire body. Patches were visible on her pink shirt – a neat wet line beneath each breast. She had a real disco fanny. She had forgotten to wear a panty liner, and was worried that she had wet herself and that it might have seeped through to the crotch of her jeans.

"Who are you to talk to me about consequences?" Jim said. "What have you ever done that has any? What risks have you ever taken? You're a boring ugly do-gooding nobody. You're a waste of space. The most exciting thing you've ever done is meet me. You're barely even alive."

With this, Jim stood up slowly, scrunched

his homework into a tiny ball, threw it across the room directly into the small wastepaper basket in the corner, and left.

How did Eileen get through the rest of the session? To this day, she'll never know. But somehow she managed to talk about Rab's attempt to murder some kid with a machete until the two hours of group work were over.

And how did she write the breach report so fast? Within twenty minutes, the following document was typed, copied, in its envelope, and ready to deliver to court.

## Breach of Probation for Failure to Comply

**Name of Probationer:** *James Bain*

**Name of Supervising Officer:** *Eileen McDonald*

### Basis of Report

*This report is based on my knowledge of Jim Bain as his Supervising Officer for the past nine months. During that time, I have attempted to see Mr Bain on a weekly basis, either in group work* sessions, one-to-one office interviews or home visits. Mr Bain has, however, failed to appear for appointments on two occasions and has often been very late without valid reasons (see reasons for breach below).

### Personal circumstances

Jim Bain continues to live alone in a furnished flat for the homeless on the 14th floor of a high rise flat in the Gorbals area of Glasgow. His grandfather, with whom he had lived since he was born, and to whom he was very close, died when he was thirteen years old, and this appears to have affected him very badly. At the age of thirteen, Mr Bain moved from his grandfather's house to his parents' home in the Gorbals, and was sent to a new secondary school. He had excelled at his last school, but soon after his arrival at Shaw Academy, he began to truant and misbehave and he was suspended twice. When Mr Bain was fifteen years old, his father died from liver failure. His mother died of lung cancer soon after. He does not recall them with any love, referring to them as the "Jakies". At fifteen, Mr Bain was found living in very poor conditions in his parents' house. He was taken into care. He often ran away from children's *homes and his career in stealing cars began to develop. Mr Bain has continued to steal cars on a regular basis since the age of fifteen, and left school at the age of sixteen having passed no formal exams.*

*He has no family and seems to be a loner, attending no clubs and having no particular hobbies or interests. He is single at the moment and states he has never had a long term relationship.*

*He has not attempted to find a job. He insists he "has his own plan" and does not need help to find employment. He has refused to explain this plan to me.*

*Mr Bain states that he does not use illegal drugs. I have no information as to whether he is speaking the truth.*

### Response to probation

*Mr Bain has not responded well to social work supervision. He has failed to attend two office appointments (see copies of first and second written warnings attached). He has also twice been late for group work (see dates attached). To add to this, he has been disruptive and rude in group work sessions, defying group rules by swearing and refusing to complete homework (see dates attached).*

**Conclusion**

*Mr Bain has not co-operated with my instructions as his supervising officer. Despite my many attempts to assist him to work on his offending behaviour, he is not motivated to do so. As a result, I feel there is no choice but to recommend that the probation order is ended. Mr Bain has already made use of most of the community based options available, and these do not appear to have worked. Indeed, his failure to comply with the orders of the court indicates that he has no respect for the law and no intention of becoming law abiding. As a result, I respectfully suggest that there is no option left for Mr James Bain but custody.*

**EILEEN MCDONALD**

**CRIMINAL JUSTICE SOCIAL WORKER**

*Little rat*, Eileen thought, as she told the receptionist she would deliver this one to court by hand.

The little rat.

# Chapter 4

## Factors Leading Up To The Crime

Eileen was feeling angry. So angry she wanted to swear out loud. Would she do it? Would she say 'bloody hell' out loud? She had never sworn, nor yelled, nor burped, nor farted (except in the toilet). Her father had taught her to have manners. If she placed her elbow on the table, or spoke with her mouth full, he would recite the following poem:

*"The Goops, they lick their fingers*
*And the Goops, they lick their knives:*
*They spill their broth on the table cloth*

*Oh, they lead disgusting lives."*

In the same way Richard was anti-Goop. He wanted women to behave like ladies. And Eileen was happy to do so. In fact, the strict weekly menu they still stuck to had been her idea. She had written it up in the third month of their marriage, sticking it proudly to the fridge as part of her new role as wife and household manager, a role she'd hoped would soon be joined by mother.

Sometimes Eileen tasted a small spurt of bile when the young offenders or her colleagues let rip with swear words or body gas and once – when Richard farted in his sleep – Eileen had had to retreat to the bathroom to take some air and wash her face. It upset her so much that it made her ill. Eileen was proud to be traditional, sensitive and polite.

But now, she felt like yelling at the top of her lungs and she may have done so if she didn't have more important things to do with her energy.

She had a report to deliver.

And she had to buy mince.

The cheapest mince nearby was in a butcher shop across the river. It wasn't safe to carry purses or handbags in this part of town, so Eileen put her keys and her five pound note in the front pocket of her jeans, the folded envelope containing the breach report in the back pocket, and made her way towards the city.

*What risks have I ever taken?* Eileen thought as she walked over the suspension bridge connecting the Gorbals with the city centre. She'd never bungee-jumped off a bridge. She'd never dived head first into the deep end of a pool. She'd never had a one night stand, or any unplanned sex for that matter. Even with Alex, her first and only pre-Richard lover, their three sexual adventures were planned to the tee. "Meet me behind the tennis shed," he'd say, and she'd obey, as she always obeyed.

It was no different with Richard. "Now," he'd say and she'd prepare to undress.

*Goodness*, Eileen thought as she wandered along the Clyde and turned into a small curved side street filled with an odd mixture of shops,

*I've never even had a child. Bloody lazy ovaries. Bloody early menopause.*

Eileen watched as the cheerful fifty-something butcher bagged her pound of mince.

Then she spotted it. A recently opened retro clothes shop across the road.

"New shop, that's good," she said, as she dug into her pocket and handed over her five pound note.

"Aye, if you're built like Kylie," the young customer behind her said.

"I'm not much older, you know." Several sets of eyebrows rose at Eileen's pathetic response.

Leaving the butcher's shop, change in pocket, bag of mince in carrier bag in hand, Eileen stopped and looked around her. Why was everybody either pregnant or pram-pushing? They were everywhere, the mothers, smiling at their children, rubbing their fat bellies, offering cartons of orange juice to their darlings.

She shook her head and walked past four workmen who were sunbathing beside a large

34

hole in the road. Someone wolf whistled. Eileen remembered back to when she was in her early twenties. Men wolf whistled her all the time then, most of all if she was wearing her tennis skirt. It had annoyed her at the time. She used to snarl at the men, tell them to please behave like gentlemen. This time, she smiled and turned around to reply to the compliment. She soon wished she hadn't.

"No' you!" the whistler yelled at her as he spotted her nodding her thanks. The other workmen laughed. Everyone else in the street seemed to stop and laugh. Eileen saw everything in slow motion. They had whistled at the eighteen-year-old girl walking out of the retro clothes shop. The girl had a mini skirt on. She had long straight legs like Eileen used to have: thin ankles, no veins, no long dark brown hair, no yellowish liver spots. The eighteen-year-old had a bag from the new shop, filled with sexy youthful purchases that would make men whistle at her for the following twelve years or so. When one of the men whistled again with a "Hey, darling!" the eighteen-year-old told him to get a life.

Eileen needed to breathe. She needed to control her emotions. She ignored the staring, laughing people. She rocked back and forth until the anger went away and looked once more at the shop. It was bright red, outside and in. She hadn't noticed this before. It seemed to throb with sensuality and fertility. It beckoned her to come in, come in, be one with me, now.

# Chapter 5

Eileen was feeling excited. She was walking towards the shop. Her heart was racing. Her head was hot. She couldn't feel her legs. They were moving without her telling them to, walking in the door, along the worn floorboards towards a rack of clothes once made for models, now worn again by models.

The shop assistant gossiped to a friend on the phone. She had a nose piercing. She wore a fantastic, tight geometric patterned dress. Eileen noticed a similar dress on the rack near the till.

"We only go up to a size 12," the woman said, taking time out from her important chat about some guy called Jerry who looked fab in and out of uniform and was going to meet her later and was definitely, definitely, telling his wife on the weekend.

"Lovely," Eileen grunted, putting the dress back, moving to a clothes rack at the back of the shop and picking up a pair of flared high-waisted jeans. She almost put them back down – weren't low cut jeans the thing nowadays? She'd bought her pair from Marks hoping so. But as she turned to replace the item, she saw a poster of Kylie Minogue on the wall. Kylie was wearing high-waisted jeans. They almost reached her tiny ribs. They had fabulous buttons in the fly area like the ones in Eileen's hand. They flared to the floor with a dramatic sweep. They looked cutting edge, stunning.

The changing room was upstairs. Eileen took the size 12 jeans and walked to the second floor. It was smaller than the ground floor shop area, but even more glorious. Red velvet curtains adorned the huge bay window. Racks of wonderful multi-coloured gear edged the boarded room. Music blared from the speakers. There was no shop assistant up there, and no other customers.

Eileen opened the thick golden curtain of the changing room. Closing it behind her, she was struck dumb by the image of herself in the 360 degree mirror. Oh, Lordy, she looked terrible. Her pink stretch shirt (also M & S) was too small for her and although the under-boob sweat patches had dried, there was now a tell-tale white-brown stain to remind her. If she bent down, large greying stomach-control underpants filled the gap between the top of her jeans and the bottom of her shirt. Her bra could be seen through the shirt, from the back and the front, flesh oozing from its straining straps. As for her jeans, they were the ugliest jeans she had ever seen. The wrong colour – too light. The wrong length – too short. The wrong cut – through the thick denim you could actually make out the bubbles of her cellulite. The wrong shape – too low. (My, when she stretched both hands to the ceiling, her large greying stomach control underpants pinged down over the fly so that they no longer concealed her flabby stomach. Worse still, greying pubic hair now popped out above them).

The image made her dizzy. She was a fat, frumpy old lump. She was an uncool, ugly frump. She was ... Oh God, she was really dizzy. The 360 degree mirror was too much. The light, though kindly and dim, was too bright. The room too small. White spots floated before her eyes. Blood drained from her face. Then suddenly, a super-fire, the kind that kills people in Australia every summer, the kind that hurls 100 feet high and travels over 100 miles an hour, rocketed towards her face. The heat was unbearable. She swayed. She was going to faint. She started seeing things ...

*An enormous pair of tweezers plucking an enormous thick black hair from her chin.*

*The doctor, leaning in, saying, "I'm afraid it's not pregnancy, Mrs McDonald."*

*Richard, sensually rubbing raw minced meat into her stomach, cooing, "You are gorgeous, so you are! Yes you are!"*

*Jim Bain saying, "Better than sex. You ever felt*

*like that ... You're barely even alive."*

*Moppet, licking her, oh, God, don't imagine that, not there, no.*

Eileen needed to breathe. She ripped her jeans and shirt and cardigan off.

She was now naked except for her large underpants and undersized bra. She put her hands over her face to check it was true, and it was, she was burning alive.

And then, something happened.

The music changed.

Kylie Minogue. Na na na, na na na na na. Or la la la, la la la la la. It was hard to tell which. Kylie was singing to her, speaking to her. It was as if that wonderful woman, her peer – oh yes – had come into the changing room with a large rubber fire hose and put out her facial flames.

Clear and cool now, Eileen began to put the high-waisted flared jeans on. It was worth the effort as she pulled them over her calves, over her knees, wrenched, yanked, heaved, over her thighs, and up, up, oh so high, over her belly button, all the way to her ribs. The zip complied more easily than she'd expected. And the button only needed a few tugs before it was near its hole, sideways, through its hole, right in, done.

Ah.

She looked up slowly and when she caught the image before her, she wasn't at all surprised. She was beautiful. She was fresh. She was slim. She was cutting edge. She was stunning. As stunning as Kylie Minogue.

She said this out loud. *"I am as stunning as Kylie Minogue."*

Then, more loudly, *"I AM as sexy as Kylie Minogue."*

And then she danced.

The song got louder. And better. More beautiful. Her movements were graceful and sexy as she whisked her body around the four by four changing room. She forgot everything else. She forgot the lonely childhood with a mother who cried most days and a father who demanded silence at dinner. She forgot the weeks of crying herself to sleep in the dormitory wondering what other nine-year-old children were doing (snuggling into bed with their parents after a bad dream, perhaps?). She forgot the few joyous years of freedom following school, when she played tennis and laughed and knew she was pretty and wanted to help people, make a difference, change the world. Then there had been twenty long years of marriage to Richard, who year by year stiffened into a carbon copy of her barrister father while she and her lazy ovaries rotted away like a doormat that has been bashed by years of feet rubbing and relentless rain. She thought of none of these things. She thought of nothing at all. Everything was movement and sound and pure, pure joy.

It was na na na, not la la la and she wished it could go on forever but sadly, it stopped. As fast as she could, Eileen changed back into her own clothes, which would from now on represent the old her, and walked downstairs.

"Can you hold these for me till tomorrow?" Eileen asked, putting the high-waisted jeans on the counter.

"One moment," the shop assistant said,

still talking on the phone. She was discussing having the CCTV mended. "Tomorrow morning, OK," she said. "We've been without it for one night and it's not safe. We need it up and running by the end of tomorrow. 9am? Great. Bye."

"What was that?" the shop assistant said after hanging up.

"I was wondering if you could hold these for me till tomorrow, please," Eileen said.

"I'm afraid we don't hold things," the shop assistant said, worried that someone as uncool as Eileen might display something she had bought in the shop in public.

But Kylie had set Eileen alight. She wasn't going to let this woman put her down. She took the jeans back to the rack and wondered what she should do next. She only had a few coins left after she'd bought the mince – not even enough to replace the sandwich Richard had given to Moppet that morning. And there was only one pair of these. One of a kind. If she didn't buy them now, she might lose them. Oh, if only Richard had put her name on the bank account like she'd asked. She could scoot over to the cash machine and withdraw some money, like most people do.

"We've got some mutton in," Eileen heard the shop assistant say into the receiver in the background.

*Mutton?* Eileen said to herself, gritting her teeth and feeling the fire return to her face. How dare she? This time, the fire did not make Eileen dizzy or faint, it urged her on. And instead of meekly replacing the jeans on the hanger and being sorry that she even existed she just waited for the hot flush to subside. Then Eileen found herself walking up the stairs, into the changing room and closing the golden curtains behind her.

# Chapter 6

## The Crime

Eileen hadn't exactly thought this out in advance. She hadn't planned to pull the high-waisted jeans back on and clip her own tired denims on the shop's hanger. She hadn't told herself – *Eileen, now what you are going to do is walk slowly out of the changing room, down the stairs, and calmly hang your old jeans on the rack. Then, Eileen, you are going to hold your head high and walk right past that rude young thing at the till and dance out of the door.*

How could she have made such a plan in

advance when her heart was pounding more loudly than the Eminem track now playing on the stereo? When her body was buzzing like that bee last Wednesday that had zzzzzzzed around the bed head while Richard did his thing? When her face and hands and legs were bursting with pleasure that she had never felt before, and certainly not when she and Richard were having sex?

The shop assistant didn't flinch as Eileen slipped past her. Eileen didn't either. She looked right ahead, chin up, confident and assured, until she had left the shop.

It was cloudy and the cold Glasgow air roused her senses. The pregnant ladies, the mothers with prams, the eighteen-year-old in the mini skirt, had all gone. The workmen were no longer resting but working in their hole. She wouldn't care if they laughed at her now. How could she care when the most glorious garment in the world had made its way onto her legs?

She liked the fact that it was hard to walk – one thick thigh curving around the other, cuffs scuffing the ground beneath her M & S ballet-style pumps. It *shouldn't* be easy to look this good. She found herself bounding towards the end of the street and then full on dancing over the suspension bridge. She was a funky woman in a funky town. Her arms were alive! If there'd been a bungee lead on the side of the bridge, she'd have strapped her ankles to it and leaped right on over. If there'd been a good looking pastry chef coming at her from the other direction, she'd have grabbed his hands and whirled him round and round. His white hat would have flown from his head and they would have laughed. (Eileen had a thing about chocolate chip cookies and the men who might make them.) Was she skipping now? Indeed she was, all the way to the front of the Sheriff Court, skipping and twirling and laughing. Ha!

She didn't wait to get her breath back before bounding up the stairs, past the solicitors, witnesses and offenders, and into the court social work office.

"Hello there," Eileen said as the glass barrier slid open. The social worker behind the window was a woman she knew from

University. They'd done their Diploma together. "Hello, Louise, how are you?"

Louise didn't recognise her. It was probably her newfound image that threw her, Eileen thought. "Eileen McDonald. Well, I was Eileen Hopkin back then. You remember? We did the criminal justice course together at Jordanhill."

"Ah, Eileen, yes. Did you ever get to Africa?"

Back then, Eileen had been planning to head overseas after the course. "No. I got married. You know how it goes."

"Well it's nice to see you again. You're looking ... healthy."

*Healthy*. Why did people never say what they really meant when they described her and her life? Just say it, she thought ... *You're looking fat*. If Eileen didn't feel so Goddamn sexy, she'd have been rather upset by this comment.

"You got a report for us?"

"Of course. Here it is," Eileen said. "An urgent one. Can you get it to the clerk today?"

"No problems," Louise said, watching as Eileen realised that the report she'd written after the group work session, the report she'd typed and copied and folded and enveloped, the report that would send young Jim Bain to jail, was not there.

She reached round to her other back pocket and as she did it dawned on her.

The report was in the back pocket of her M & S jeans, the jeans she had hung on the rack of the retro clothing shop a few minutes earlier.

"Are you OK?" Louise asked, wondering if Eileen's grey frozen face indicated the onset of a heart attack or stroke.

It was as if the spirit of Kylie had been swiftly driven out, a twist of smoke sucked from her body, leaving the old Eileen standing in the court social work office, her mouth wide open with horror. Not only had she left the breach of conduct report – with her name typed clearly in black ink on the top – but she had also left her set of keys, the ones which had the precious spare to Richard's new bike.

"Are you all right?" Louise asked, but Eileen had already fled the office.

*Oh Lordy, Oh Lordy, Oh Lordy*, Eileen thought as she huffed and puffed her way across the suspension bridge. The shop assistant might know already. She might have phoned the police. And what would Richard say? "You did what, woman? You *lost* my key when I specially asked you to be careful, when I made you responsible for looking after it?" He'd go all silent, like when she forgot to defrost the lamb chops that time, refusing to talk to her till she'd proved that her microwave could do the job and delay their Thursday dinner by only ten minutes.

What on earth had she been thinking? She was mad. She was an idiot. Her hormones had turned her brain to mush. There were good reasons for never taking risks, good reasons for rules, laws, limits. And certain things follow on if you disobey them: guilt, punishment, and the anger of bosses, husbands, parents, society, God. Eileen smashed into the back of one of the workmen as she turned into the side street. He called her a fat cow. She apologised, then stopped at the side of the clothes shop and, with only one eye, carefully looked into the window.

There were no police. The shop assistant was on the phone, her mind miles away. Thank God.

She took three deep breaths, then entered the shop, walking to the rack at the back. She could see her shapeless jeans from several feet away. They were there! She walked slowly, getting closer, and reached a trembling hand towards the pockets ...

"Excuse me!" Eileen jumped, turned round. The shop assistant was right behind her. She had a snide look on her face. She was nearly six feet tall. Her angry eyes were narrow slits.

"I think you forgot something," said the shop assistant.

# Chapter 7

Running full pelt and pushing the
shoulder of the tall rude woman from the till,
she dashed out through the front door of the
shop, along the street, past the workmen's
hole, round the corner and deep into the city.
Eileen was running so fast she didn't notice
the shop assistant following her to the door of
the shop, holding the bag of mince she'd left
in the changing room and looking puzzled as
the fat woman sprinted clumsily to the left.
Eileen didn't see the shop assistant shrug,
throw the mince in the green wheelie bin in
the lane next to the shop, and go back inside

to carry on with her telephone conversation. Eileen didn't notice because she had to be an athlete now. Athletes notice nothing. They are machines. They run.

Who was she kidding? After one block a stitch was splitting her stomach in half, breathing was a thing of the past, and her size 12 stolen jeans were protesting against the movement of the size 14 (OK, so 16) legs they encased. Bending over to ease the stitch, she gasped several times before looking up again. There, right in front of her, was a policeman. An hour earlier, the world had been filled with fertile women and men who found her sexually repulsive. Now it seemed to be filled with policemen. This officer was looking right at her. He was walking towards her. He had a determined look on his face. He knew. She knew he knew. He knew she knew he knew. She ran across the road, through the red pedestrian light. A car tooted, just missed her. "Hey!" the officer yelled, so she ran faster, along the main shopping street, pushing past shoppers as they browsed the city streets, racing past businessmen, another police officer. Holy Lord, a siren.

It was clear they were coming for her. She ran to the end of the pedestrian strip, into a dark lane, to the end, left into another lane, darker still, and left into another. The siren was getting louder. Oh Lordy, oh Lordy.

A wheelie bin. She puffed her way towards the bin, stood on the pile of newspapers beside it, and jumped inside. The revolting smell of the half filled container made her retch. She closed her eyes and prayed.

*Dear God, please don't let them find me. I'm sorry. I'm bad and I'm sorry. I'm stupid and I'm sorry. I'm fat and old and useless and I'm sorry. Please don't let them find me.*

Had the siren stopped? At least it had faded. Minutes passed like hours. She was breathing again. How long had she been holding her breath? All was silent. She'd managed to lose the police officer. She gently lifted the lid of the bin open. Her cat-like eyes peered from the crack. Someone was talking nearby.

Shutting the lid again, she grasped the rubbish beside her legs and held her breath. Something sticky, something wet, something soft and squidgy in a plastic bag. After ten minutes or so, she felt confident to take a look outside again. An inch was enough for her to see that the lane was empty. All was silent. The lane was right beside the retro clothing shop. A policeman with a truncheon was walking towards the shop. "Hey, Jerry," the shop assistant said, letting him in and closing the door behind them.

Bang. She shut it. How had she been so stupid to run full circle and end up at the scene of her crime? And now the officer was inside. Was he taking her details? Looking through her old jeans? Radioing base to get a team around to her house and her office *now*? Eileen could see her future clear as day.

*You're fired, Mrs McDonald.*

*Five years seven months, Mrs McDonald.*

*We don't like probation officers here in B Hall, Mrs McDonald.*

*Your parents have suggested you take them off*

*your visitors list, Mrs McDonald.*

*You are no longer Mrs McDonald, Mrs McDonald.*

She decided to wait in the bin until the shop was closed and the officer and the shop assistant had gone home. She held the lid tight from the inside to stop passers-by from opening it. She cried. She prayed. The space in her stomach that should have been filled with a ham sandwich rumbled. She jumped in fear at every single noise: a door shutting, people talking, machinery humming, a bird cooing, footsteps scraping, a car parking, the click of a lock, more footsteps.

It had been several hours. Her legs were aching. The high waist of her ridiculous jeans (she knew that now) was cutting into her ribs. She had lost the feeling in her left arm, which was probably good because if she'd been able to feel her left arm she'd have known that it was now covered in the ooze from some baby's soiled nappy.

*This is where I belong*, Eileen sobbed. *I belong with baby poo and potato peels and empty beer cans and God what is that on my neck? Sticky and slimy and this is where I belong. Used, finished, empty, disgusting. I am waiting to be land fill.*

# Chapter 8

Jim's grandpa had been a mechanic. He'd lived in a house out past Rutherglen and worked in a garage in Polmadie. After he lost his wife ("the greatest woman there ever was," he would often say to Jim, "God knows how she had that useless father of yours for a son."), he decided to save enough money to buy his own business. "We can run it together, son. Not in this wet hellhole, but somewhere sunny. I'm thinking of Majorca."

Jim used to love helping his gramps out after school, lying on the ground beside him, handing him this tool and that, or sitting in the car turning the engine on and off when directed.

One evening, when Jim was thirteen, his grandfather went out to the garage and rolled under an old Ford to work on the suspension.

"Gramps?" Jim said. "Tea's ready!" (Jim, at thirteen, made a mean lamb curry.)

His grandfather didn't answer.

"Gramps? Two minutes! I'm gonnae serve up."

Jim went inside the house, served the dinner, then came back out to the garage. His gramps' feet had not moved. When he rolled under the car beside him, Jim saw that he was dead. He had died with a spanner in his hand. At the funeral, the minister said he had died doing what he loved doing. *Did he, hell*, Jim had thought. *He died dying. He died trying not to die.* So what? he felt like yelling at the black-clad minister, you think he was enjoying the pain in his chest, you think he was loving trying to get a breath in and not being able to? You think he enjoyed trying to yell for help but not being able to?

Jim's grandfather had saved five grand, almost enough to get the business in Majorca going. The day after the funeral, Jim found it in a shoebox on the top shelf of his gramps' clothes cupboard. The next day he tried to hide it under his new bed in his new home. Sadly, his father caught him and within two years, he had spent it all on drink.

Jim refused to give up on the dream. OK, so maybe his gramps wouldn't have liked the way he earned money – stealing Robin Hood style – ("Robin Hood, my arse!" his gramps would have said, wagging his finger) and selling to this guy down by the Clyde. But how else could he escape the hell he'd been dumped in? What choice did he have but to use the only skills he had to make a fresh start?

He was almost there. He'd saved ten grand in two years.

But now that fat cow had threatened to send him back to court. He decided he had to leave at once. He bought a fake passport from a guy down at the Arches. He bought a ferry ticket to Spain. All he needed was one last set of wheels, not to sell, but to get him there.

So Jim was feeling excited. He was dreaming of zooming off like Steve McQueen in *The Great Escape*. In fact, he'd been looking for a big shiny monster bike all over the city, when a Bentley Continental (British Racing Green) drove through the Salt Market and into a side street. He watched the smart arsehole lock it and walk away, briefcase in hand, and then took a deep breath. OK, so maybe he wouldn't escape on a bike, maybe not like Steve McQueen. This might have to do.

Jim could feel the changes in his body. Blood was making its way to the tools he needed – to his legs, to get over there; to his hands, to get it open; to his fingers, to get it started. His face was burning hot. His breathing was sharp. He was a bull. He was shuffling the dirt with his left hoof. There was a red flag and it was making everything around him slow down, slow down. It was the moment before the charge.

He looked around him. No one. He sniffed the air, scraped the ground with his right foot, took out a wedge and a bent piece of wire from his pocket, walked towards the car, and sized up the job.

"Jim?"

He jumped, turned around. But he couldn't see anyone. As he'd thought, the lane was empty, except for a pigeon eating scraps beside the bin.

"Over here!" said the voice.

Jim walked closer to the pigeon, stared at it, puzzled, as it nibbled crumbs. A talking pigeon. He shouldn't have had that second spliff. It had happened before a couple of times, the visions. Once, after a night on the Red Bull, vodka, skunk and eccies (which did not make him a junkie), he'd seen his grandfather clear as day, standing beside him as he hurled the contents of his stomach into the toilet. His grandfather was wagging a finger, saying "You shouldnae of done that, son."

His grandfather had been dead twelve months at the time. Bloody selfish bastard, dying like that and forcing him to move back home with his screwed up parents.

"In here!" said the voice, bringing him back to the present. It was a female voice, not his grandfather's.

He walked closer to the pigeon, leaned down until his face was inches from it. "You're not talking. You're a pigeon."

"No. Up here!" Jim looked up from the nibbling bird and noticed a pair of eyes peering out from a crack in the lid of the wheelie bin. He moved closer, lifted the lid slowly and saw his probation officer covered in gunge.

"Jesus Christ!" he yelled, banging the lid shut. Was this like that other time when he was hurtling along the M8 at 70mph and his grandpa suddenly appeared in the passenger seat, shaking his head, saying, "You shouldn't be doing this, son." Was it? Or was the old cow really in the bin? He was mulling it over when the lid opened again.

"It's me, Eileen. Please, Jim … I need a favour."

# Chapter 9

Eileen had arranged a deal once before. It went like this:

EILEEN: *Eating grilled fish and oven chips (Wednesday) and handing Richard some leaflets about adoption.* There are so many unwanted children, Richard. Have a read of these.

RICHARD: Glancing at the leaflets. Have I ever bought a second hand car?

EILEEN: Well, no, but...

RICHARD: Have I ever shopped at Oxfam?

EILEEN: I tell you what, all you have to do is read over them. They're not cars or clothes.

RICHARD: If I read them will you stop going on about it?

And that was her only deal so far. After Richard had taken the leaflets to read, she felt pleased. She lay awake in bed that night dreaming that Richard's study was a nursery, imagining that a heart-jolting cry had woken her and she'd walked sleepily towards the baby (Anna or Charlie) that loved and needed her more than anything in the entire world.

Eileen went window shopping every day for a week after that. She picked out the wallpaper for the nursery (a yellow one, dotted with adorable teddies that would do for a boy or a girl). She chose a white painted cot and a multi-coloured fish mobile that swung round to the tune of *Twinkle Twinkle*. She decided on a three-wheeled pram she could jog with (the baby would help her lose weight!) and a buggy that folded to the size of a small suitcase.

Richard returned the leaflets seven days after receiving them. "Have I ever considered wearing a wig?" he said.

Richard was never very good at changing his mind.

She would do better at working out a deal this time. She had to.

"So what you're saying is you want me to break into a fuckin' shop ..." Jim said.

"No swearing."

"This is hardly the time and place to be preaching ground rules ... You want me to break into a shop and get your jeans."

"In a nutshell, yes."

"Why should I? Anyhow, I can't. I won't. I'm very busy."

"I won't send the report," Eileen said quickly, thinking on her feet.

"Hmm, let me think." Jim thought about it for a minute or two, then added, "Right, no breach report now or till the end of my order."

"I can't do anything if you offend again," Eileen said.

"I won't offend again, but you won't see me again either. You tell the Sheriff I came every week, that I behaved like a saint. You've never seen a criminal turn himself round like I did. You write this for the Sheriff when the order's finished and we have ourselves a deal."

Eileen was desperate. She had no choice. She was about to accept the terms. "... Plus a cash sum," Jim added.

"I don't have any money."

Jim started to walk away. Frantic, Eileen yelled after him. "OK, OK. I'll do my best."

# Chapter 10

Jim was used to doing deals. When the social worker found him living alone at fifteen, with both parents well dead, he insisted on being handed over to that pretty key worker at the children's home and won. When the Sheriff accused him of a list of Road Traffic Offences, he pleaded the hard luck story. He had no one to love him when he left care. So he managed to get a twelve-month probation order (with a condition to attend group work).

When Mandy, the dark-haired girl from the high rise next to his refused to go out to a film, he persuaded her to meet him for a drink.

OK, so she left with her mates after he'd paid for all their Bacardi and Cokes, but he'd still taken her out. And now, he would not be sent back to court, he could vanish to the life he and his gramps dreamed of, and would even get some cash into the bargain. Piece of cake.

They waited till it was dark. Eileen stayed inside the bin, and Jim hid behind it until the shop assistant and her police officer came out of the store.

"Sorry about the truncheon, Jerry," the shop assistant said, patting the officer's bottom as he tucked in his shirt.

"Oy, not out here in the street," he said.

"And you'll tell her this weekend?" she added as they walked past the bin.

"Don't push it, woman," the officer replied, trying to open the lid of the bin to throw his used condom inside. The lid would not budge. He pulled harder. It was stuck. Inside, Eileen's fingernails were grasping the lid with all their might. After two attempts, the officer gave up and threw his condom beside the bin. It landed on Jim's arm. Jim, with a grunt of disgust, watched the secret couple walk down the lane and go round opposite corners.

"Oh, my God!" Jim screamed when they'd gone. "I've got pig spunk on me." He grabbed some newspaper and wiped the condom off his shoulder, then knocked on the lid. "They're away. And don't worry, he wasn't in the shop about you."

Eileen opened the lid and started to stand up. "Get back down! Stay in there," Jim ordered. "And hold tight."

# Chapter 11

Eileen had been on the ghost train as a child. She found it terrifying, moving in the darkness towards unknown horrors. This felt the same. For some reason, Jim was moving the bin with her in it. "What are you doing?" she asked as she bumped slowly in the darkness.

"Shut up. Who's the expert here, eh?"

She closed her eyes, held tight and placed her trust in Jim Bain, seventeen, lean, five foot eleven, curly dark hair, gleaming white teeth. *He'd be good looking if he liked himself and got a bit of sun*, Eileen thought, the rubbish jumping about her as the bin bumped backwards, away from the shop and then stopped.

"Right, on the count of three, hold on tight," Jim said, and Eileen did as she was told. After all, Jim stole things all the time. He would have nifty gadgets attached to a special work belt around his waist. He would have already worked out his strategy, planned it to a tee, like Michael Cain in *The Italian Job* or George Clooney in *Ocean's Eleven*.

"One ... Two ..." Jim said. Eileen held her breath and grasped the top of the bin ... "Three!"

She lent back and held on as best she could as the bin clanged noisily, getting up speed as Jim pushed it forward, faster and faster. Then it banged with a thump into the window of the shop.

Ouch! Eileen's head smashed forward then back as the bin hit the window. A moment later, she opened the lid to find Jim rubbing his chin with his fingers. His cunning plan to bash the bin through the glass-fronted shop had failed. What an idiot. Eileen pushed the bin onto the ground and crawled out. The bag of mince which the assistant had chucked in there was now open and splattered on her chest.

"That was your plan?" she said angrily, wiping sludge from her face and hands. This guy was useless.

"How much do you weigh?" he asked.

"Eleven and a half stone."

"Really? I took you for at least fifteen."

"Cheers ... Twelve and a half at most," Eileen huffed, rubbing down the legs of the new trousers that had most likely ruined her life.

"Can you not pick the lock or something?" Eileen said.

"I only steal cars. You should know that."

Eileen looked around her and nodded towards the Bentley Jim had been eyeing earlier on.

Jim looked at the car, and then at Eileen. "You know how much these are worth?" Jim asked. "You don't go smashing these sweet babies into shop windows."

"You got a better idea?"

Jim sighed, walked over to the car, stroked the bonnet as if saying sorry and placed a small wedge in the crack of the door to pry it open a little. He retrieved the bent piece of wire from his pocket for a second time, slid it through the crack and wiggled it around for what seemed like hours until the door finally opened.

The car siren blared as Jim jumped in, fiddled about, opened the hood, got out, fiddled about again, jumped back into the driver's seat, fiddled some more, and finally started the car. "Out of the way!" he yelled, revving hard before backing back as far as he could and driving full force into the shop window.

Eileen froze on the spot as glass shattered and the car alarm joined forces with the shop alarm, screaming for the police to arrive. She might never have moved if Jim hadn't rushed towards her, grabbed her arm and told her to get a move on.

It was dark inside the shop. Glass crunched underfoot. Eileen felt her way past the till, past the rack of geometric patterned dresses next to it, towards the back of the shop, until she at last found the jeans rack at the rear. She fumbled with hangers. Jeans fell to the ground.

"Move it! Move it!" Jim yelled. "You've got two minutes tops."

Another siren began to wail, must be a police vehicle making its way towards them, getting louder.

Eileen clawed at clothes with her shaky hands. She had never felt so terrified as she groped at one pair of jeans, with a label. Not hers. Another, fallen to the ground now, too hard. A three-quarter length pair, nup. Skinny jeans. Teensy jeans. Then – at last – a pair that felt as only hers would feel: cheap, nasty, lived-in, stretched. They felt ugly. And their pockets were bulging.

As the siren outside got louder, Eileen unclipped her jeans from the hanger, rushed to the broken window of the shop and jumped into the driver's side of the Bentley.

"Get in!" she yelled to Jim.

The lights of the police car could be seen at the end of the lane now. And although Jim did not want to get in the car with Eileen at the wheel, he had no choice. He got in, shut the door, and watched as his probation officer turned the key and reached for her seat belt.

"Forget that!" Jim yelled.

Eileen fumbled, unable to forget her lifetime seatbelt habit. Clicking the belt into place, she pressed her foot on the clutch, clunked the gears clumsily into first, and revved the engine gently with a trembling foot.

"Get a move on! They're here! Hurry up!" he yelled.

Jim watched as Eileen suddenly transformed into a new woman, one who was no longer a boring fat cow, no longer terrified, but a feisty, angry, adrenalin-filled madwoman who backed into the lane and did a 90 degree turn so fast that the vehicle skidded in mince and nappies, and left a cloud of debris as it tore towards the main street, the police tailing her twenty feet behind.

# Chapter 12

*I am Eileen McDonald*, this new woman said to herself. *I am 45. I am beautiful. I am not land fill. I am driving faster than anyone has ever driven. I will lose the cops on my tail by driving across the Clyde at 130 miles an hour, by driving down the taxi lane in Pollokshaws Road at 130 miles per hour, by changing gear, turning, driving down Clarkston Road at 125 miles per hour, the cops out of sight now as I drive, at 135 miles per hour, out towards East Kilbride, right over those stupid roundabout bumps in my way. In open countryside, I will skid off the road, bumping over scrub, only just missing trees, stopping the engine* to wait, hidden by bushes and darkness, until the sirens have gone, and the helicopter overhead has given up and gone off to hover in other parts. I am Eileen McDonald and I am not thinking about anything but driving, with the roof down now as my passenger has pressed a button and opened it. The wind is rushing through my hair and who cares how it's going to look afterwards? Fourth to fifth again, tyres screeching around bends, bouncing over blind summits. I may be yelling. Am I? If I am, it's wonderful and I wish I'd done more of it. I wish I'd opened my mouth and roared when my father said a son would never have done social work, a son would never have lived in the rain in Glasgow, a son would never have been so damn useless. I wish I'd yelled when Richard told me I was so fat he had to do it from behind. I wish I'd growled at the doctor like an animal when he told me I should be happy not having to worry about women's problems any more. I wish I'd screamed when Moppet and that bike turned up to take the teensy bit of affection I used to get from the man I lived with. I am yelling. I love yelling.

# Chapter 13

"Shut up! You're scaring the living shite out of me," Jim said. "And slow down, you crazy bitch! This is a Bentley Continental and we've already bust it up. Be kind to it. Give it the respect it deserves. We lost the cops back in East Kilbride. Stop. Let me drive it."

She skidded to a halt on a dirt country road, car doors were opened, places switched, and Jim held the wheel at last.

How long did they drive like that? Jim wondered as he lazed in the sun the following day. How long did they sit silently, the air blowing over them, each with an elbow slung over the window, watching the moon slowly vanish behind dark clouds, hardly noticing towns whizz by, the water opening up to their right, the farms and the hills and the grass and the stars? How long was it? Two hours? Four? Jim didn't know. All he knew was that they were silent the entire time. And they were smiling.

# Chapter 14

Eileen had never felt like this before. As Jim parked in front of her house and turned off the engine, she could barely move with the ecstasy. Her lips had frozen into a smile. Her eyes were bright with life.

She hardly noticed Jim putting his hand under her left buttock.

"Glass," he said, taking a piece of shop window from her seat and placing it carefully in the ashtray.

"Thanks, Jim," Eileen said, picking up her old jeans from the back seat of the car and retrieving the piece of paper in the back pocket. She unfolded it and ripped it into little pieces. Then she said: "You'd better dump this car, Jim. They'll be looking for it."

"I will," Jim said, watching as his probation officer hurled the ripped breach report out of the window to be scattered by the light breeze.

"And listen, about the cash," Eileen began.

"Don't worry about it," Jim told her. "I had a blast."

Eileen took a key out of the other pocket of her old jeans and handed it to him. "I want you to take this ... wherever you're heading."

"I'll swap you ... Collect the mail and stuff, yeah?" Jim said, handing her one of the keys to his flat, then watching as Eileen got out of the car and walked towards the front door of her semi.

# Chapter 15

## The Consequences

Richard was angry. He had been walking up and down the conservatory since 6.30pm. He had no way of getting hold of his missing wife. Damned do-gooding office, shutting at five. Perhaps he should have let her have that mobile phone she'd asked for.

But something about her stopped him from yelling the questions he had prepared. Questions like:

*What time do you call this, woman?*

*Where the hell have you been?*

*How dare you?*

*I thought about phoning the hospitals!*
(Indeed he had, the thought that she'd been
killed in a crash had made him dream up all
sorts of fantasies.)

It was the look on her face that stopped
him from saying anything. A blissful calm had
taken over. He found it hard to make sense of
this look as he had never seen it on her face
before in their twenty years of marriage. (Was it
twenty? Or twenty-two? He never kept track of
such things). In the past, her face had always
worn a frozen smile that stopped short of her
eyes. *I will be happy*, her smile used to try and
say. *Things are good. I will be happy. I must be!*

It was also the smell. She was covered in a
rainbow of slime, rotting rubbish and what
looked like minced meat. She stank like week-
old prawns with nappy shit salsa.

As for those jeans, he'd never seen a
woman sliced in two like that.

What she said scared him too. More to the
point, it was what she didn't say. For example,
she didn't say:

"I'm so sorry, Richard, I was kidnapped by two men in masks in the Gorbals underground." (This would have been a good excuse, though why she would choose to get the train at the Gorbals station against his advice he would never know.)

Or: "Please forgive me, Richard, your mother phoned and she is dead." (This would also be a good excuse.)

Or: "A bus ran me over and I am badly hurt." (How badly?)

Or: "I am a bad wife. I left the mince at work and had to return there on foot because I know how it would have upset you, coming home to no mince on a Monday. But the office was locked and I couldn't get in, so I had to walk all the way to the nearest butcher which as you know is a long way away and it was closed so I had to go to the 24 hour ASDA which was out of mince." (To have forgotten it would not have been a valid excuse.)

But her face was the scariest thing about her.

"What sort of face do you call this?" he

asked as she calmly took one of his beers from the fridge, opened it and drank it down in one. "I'm listening ..."

For one moment he thought she might kill him. Perhaps this was the face of a serial killer, of a black widow just before the brutal murder. The kind of killer that can only be a woman, one whose hatred and rage builds over years and breaks out in fountains of male blood. He waited for her to move. She did, but not towards him with a knife or a gun or a rope or a cloth soaked in chloroform. She moved towards him, reached behind him for the phone, dialled a number, gave her address, and said: "One lamb bhoona, one raita, one naan, one boiled – no, make that fried – rice and one mixed pakora ... Name?"

She paused.

"My name is Eileen Hopkin."

She hung up, scrunched the empty beer can with one hand, threw it neatly into the bin in the corner, then went to the fridge and opened another.

*Right, that's enough of that*, thought

Richard. He was determined to start asking the questions he had worked out earlier in order to restore his rightful power over her.

"What time do you call this, woman?" But his voice was letting him down. It was very squeaky and unmanly.

"You should think of a better word to insult me with, Richard. 'Woman' does not do it," Eileen said, not looking at him.

At that moment, Moppet barked outside, causing Richard to start a little. Then the garage doors began to hum.

"What's that?" Richard asked.

"Sounds like the garage doors opening," Eileen replied flatly after finishing her second beer.

In a panic, Richard raced to the front window, opened it, and looked out to his left. Indeed the garage doors were opening.

"Oh, my God," he yelled as the Harley's engine revved in the garage before shooting out of the double doors, down the driveway, and then left along their street.

He ran out the front door shouting, "Stop!

Stop now! Someone help! Police! Some Ned's stolen my Harley!"

Eileen walked out calmly, stood beside him in the middle of the front garden, and waited for him to see what she could see. The green bungee lead was still tied onto the dog in the side-car and the other end was still attached to the workbench at the back of the garage, stretching, thinning and straining. Wee Moppet was looking out helplessly from her favourite new bed as it sped away at 40 then 50 then 60 miles per hour.

"Moppet!" Richard yelled too late, because the lead had reached its maximum stretch and was now returning, shooting Moppet out of the side car, high into the sky, and then down, down, towards the garage.

Richard had never been very good at catching things.

# Chapter 16

## Four months later

Eileen could feel again.

She remembered she used to do that a bit, in fact quite a lot. At the beach in Majorca, aged ten, she'd feel the warm sun prickling into her skin. In the cinema aged twenty-three, she'd feel Richard's arm hairs brush against her arm hairs. In the kitchen she'd kitted out just after the wedding, she'd feel red wine numb her veins and loud music awaken them again. Not only did the words of the song make total sense, but she could feel them deep inside her, as if she'd written them. She could have written them. Why not? She used to feel angry if a meal was bad or too expensive or if someone tooted her in their car because she was going too slowly. Not so long ago, she would have felt angry if her period came again, and the blood was as angry as she was and she'd bang the toilet door in a rage and tell God to go shove himself because what did he care, letting this happen month after month? Did he not know how much love she had to give?

And then the blood stopped altogether. And with the blood, all feeling stopped too.

But she could feel again now. No need to try to convince herself that the rain was good, that her husband was a catch, that her suburban semi was her dream home, that her job wasn't hard, that she could do without a car, a mobile phone, a baby, love. No need to pretend because for four months she had begun to feel the only thing that mattered was ...

... Hope ...

It had buzzed within her when she found

out that a lad called Antony McDade had been done with the theft of the car and of Richard's motorbike. ("He had five other Road Traffic offences, Mr McDonald," the police officer had told her angry, broken, husband. "He's a scallywag. Said he hadnae done it at first, but soon realised eight offences was much the same as five and he'd get the jail if he kept on denying he'd done them.")

And hope was present the day after, when Eileen walked into the bank and opened her very own account.

It was there when she sat opposite Richard in the lawyer's office, calmly discussing the divorce.

As she viewed flats.

As she bought a mobile phone.

As she joined the local tennis club.

As an office colleague asked her if she wanted to head out with her for lunch.

As she spoke to the agency about adopting as a single parent.

And hope was with her now as she paid one or two of Jim's bills, re-read the letter he sent her, and sat and typed a Probation Completion Report.


**Name of Probationer:** *James Bain*
**Name of Supervising Officer:** *Eileen Hopkin*


### Basis of Report

*This report is based on my knowledge of Jim Bain as his Supervising Officer for the past twelve months. During that time, I have seen Mr Bain on a weekly basis, either in group work sessions, one-to-one office interviews or during home visits.*

### Personal circumstances

*Mr Bain has continued to live in a furnished flat on the 14th floor of a high rise building in the Gorbals. Neighbours report that he keeps himself to himself and has caused no trouble in the last year. I have visited him regularly at this address, and have been impressed by how successfully Mr Bain is able to manage his own affairs. He pays his bills on time, keeps the flat neat and clean and seems determined to be independent.*

*Mr Bain now has a busy and varied life. His hobbies include painting in watercolour, swimming, fishing and watching foreign films at the cinema.*

*He is now in a long term relationship with a novelist called Ada.*

### Response to probation

*I have never worked with someone as motivated as Mr Jim Bain. All through the probation order his steady determination to be law abiding and successful has inspired the other offenders in his group.*

### Conclusion

*When Mr Bain first attended group work, he seemed cut off from the world. He was unhappy, lacking in confidence and lonely. During his period of probation, he has changed completely. He now has goals in life, and no longer blames others for his failure to achieve them. In the writer's opinion, the risk of re-offending is very low.*

**EILEEN HOPKIN**

**CRIMINAL JUSTICE SOCIAL WORKER**

Eileen put the report in the post and went

over to the group work room. Her new boys were much the same as the last lot. They sat in a semi-circle, shaking and twitching with a mixture of withdrawal and boredom.

After the warm-up exercise (every single one of them said they were feeling *all right*), Eileen stood in front of them and pointed at the felt-tipped words on her flip chart – THE OFFENCE.

"OK," Eileen said, "last week we looked at what happened before Antony committed his offences. As I explained, today we will focus on the offence itself."

As Eileen paused, Antony scratched madly at his arm.

"Antony, I want you to take yourself back. If I remember right, you stole the first vehicle – the Bentley Continental – at around 6pm on a Monday night. Free your mind. Brainstorm. It's 6pm on the night in question and you are now driving the stolen car. How are you *feeling*?"

"I dunno," Antony said, scratching himself to the point of bleeding now. "Cannae remember."

Eileen smiled, looked at Antony kindly and said, "Then I'll tell you how you feel. You feel fucking fantastic."

# About the Author

Helen FitzGerald grew up in Australia and studied English and History at the University of Melbourne. Following a period of travelling, she moved to Glasgow. She worked as a probation and parole officer for ten years before becoming a full time writer. She has written a number of novels for Faber, which have been very well received. Helen FitzGerald currently lives in Glasgow.

# Other titles in this series

### Sawbones by Stuart MacBride

They call him Sawbones: a serial killer kidnapping young women. The latest victim is Laura Jones. Sixteen years old. Pretty. Blonde. And the daughter of one of New York's most notorious gangsters. Laura's dad doesn't care about the law. Looks like Sawbones picked on the *wrong* family

### Heroes by Anne Perry

In the trenches of the First World War, men die every day. They die in their hundreds, sometimes in their thousands. But this death is different. This is cold, deliberate murder.

When men are dying around you every day, how much can one death mean? And how far can you go to avenge it?

www.barringtonstoke.co.uk